The Berenstain Bears
and
Baby Makes Five

When a brand-new cub
makes its big entrance,
it often takes a while
to get complete acceptance.

A First Time Book®

The Berenstain Bears
and
Baby Makes Five

Stan & Jan Berenstain

Random House 🏠 New York

Copyright © 2000 by Berenstain Enterprises, Inc. All rights reserved under International and Pan-American Copyright Conventions. Published in the United States by Random House, Inc., New York, and simultaneously in Canada by Random House of Canada Limited, Toronto. www.randomhouse.com/kids www.berenstainbears.com
Library of Congress Cataloging-in-Publication Data
Berenstain, Stan, 1923–   The Berenstain Bears and baby makes five /
Stan & Jan Berenstain.
    p. cm. – (First time books)
SUMMARY: Sister Bear is upset by all the attention her new baby sister is receiving.
ISBN 0-679-88960-4 (trade) — ISBN 0-679-98960-9 (lib. bdg.)
[1. Babies—Fiction.   2. Family life—Fiction.   3. Bears—Fiction.]
I. Berenstain, Jan, 1923– .   II. Title.   III. Series: Berenstain, Stan, 1923– .
First time books.   PZ7.B4483Bah   2000   99-30687
Printed in the United States of America   August 2000   10 9 8 7 6 5 4 3 2 1
RANDOM HOUSE and colophon are registered trademarks of Random House, Inc.

Big news in Bear Country!

The Bear family, who lives in the big tree house down a sunny dirt road, has a new member: a baby girl named Honey. What fun! What excitement!

What a nuisance!

Sometimes it seemed that it was
crying,

feeding,

burping,

spitting up,

and diapering around the clock.

And when it wasn't those things, it was

cuddling,

dandling,

fussing,

and kitchy-cooing.

And when it wasn't *those* things, it was
shopping, shopping, and more shopping
for things that were needed for
the new baby.

At least that's how it seemed to Sister Bear.

Brother Bear understood that babies need a lot of attention. He'd been through it before when Sister was born. But having a new baby in the house was a new experience for Sister, and she wasn't enjoying it very much.

It didn't help that when Papa came home from work every day, the first thing he did was pick up the new baby, make goo-goo eyes, and say, "How's my darlin' little dumpling?"

Dumpling. Good name for her, thought Sister—a fat little doughball that was hard to swallow.

It didn't help at all when Aunt Min and Uncle Louie visited and made a big fuss over the new baby.

"Well, Sis," said Uncle Louie, "I guess you're not the big star around here anymore. Ha-ha-ha!"

Ha-ha-ha, indeed!

It wasn't just Aunt Min and Uncle Louie. It was as if every bear for miles around came to admire the new baby and say how cute she was!

"So cute!" said Mrs. Grizzle.

"Cute as a button!" said Farmer Ben.

"Cute as a bug!" said Mrs. Bruin.

"Yeah," snapped Sister under her breath, "a *stink* bug!"
Sister had a point about the new baby being a stink bug. While she couldn't do much, she sure was good at wetting and filling diapers.

"Sister, dear," said Mama one day when she was attending to the baby, "it's not very polite to say 'pee-yoo' every time you come near the baby. Meanwhile, would you do me a favor and slosh this diaper in the toilet before you throw it away?"

"Pee-yoo!"

And the fuss they made when the baby
did the least little thing.

"Get out the tape recorder!
The baby said 'Goo'!"

"Get out the videocam!
The baby is smiling!"

"Call the newspapers!
The baby laughed out loud!"

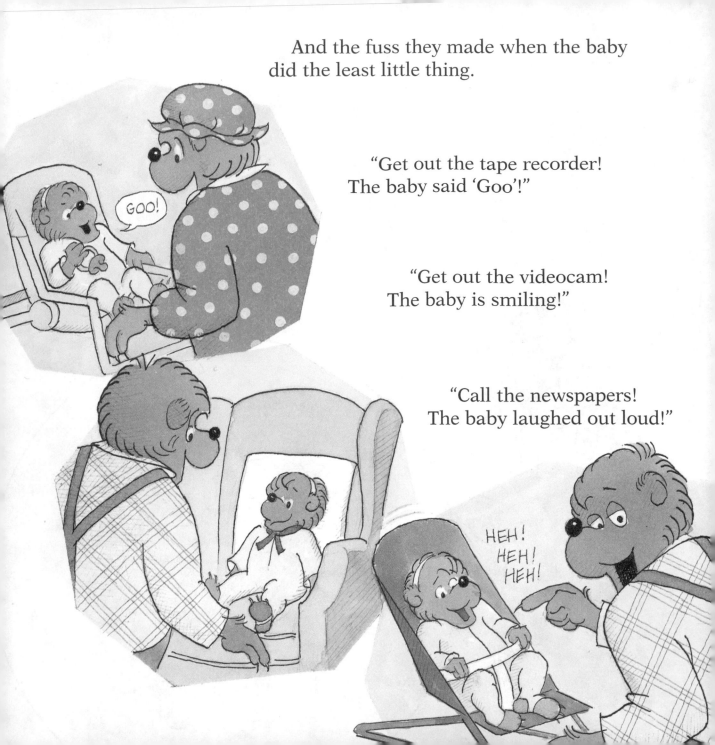

It was easy to see that Sister was getting grumpier and grumpier. At least, it would have been easy to see if Mama and Papa hadn't been so busy with the new baby.

But since babies can't do much for themselves, they do need a lot of care and attention.

Brother needed a lot of care and attention when he was a baby. So did Sister. That's the way it is with babies.

It takes Mother and Father Bluebird practically all day digging worms to feed their wide-mouthed babies.

Mother Fox works from dawn to dusk to care for and protect her kits.

Mother Kangaroo carries her joey around in her pouch until it's big enough to do proper kangaroo jumps.

Brother could tell that Sister was seriously out of sorts. She was even angry at her dolls because they reminded her of the new baby. But he had problems of his own at the time— like long division and multiplication tables.

Speaking of school, it was an assignment Sister brought home from school that told Mama that Sister wasn't exactly thrilled about the baby. Teacher Jane had asked each cub in the class to draw a picture of his or her family. Sister liked to draw. She was a very good artist.

This is what the picture looked like:

My Family

Mama   Papa   Brother Sister

When Mama saw it, she knew there was trouble afoot. "Dear," she asked, "why didn't you put your new baby sister in the picture?"

"Because," snarled Sister, "there wasn't enough room on the paper!" Then she stomped up the stairs, went into her room, and slammed the door.

Oh, dear!

That evening after the new baby was asleep, Mama had an idea. "I know what," she said. "Let's look at our videocam movies."

"Let's not and say we did," said Sister, thinking they would be the latest new baby videos.

But she couldn't have been more wrong. While that's what they looked like, that's not what they were. They were videos that Mama and Papa had taken of Sister when *she* was a baby.

They showed Papa playing kitchy-coo with her. They showed her smiling, laughing, and saying "Goo." They showed her jumping up and down in her Jumping Jack. They showed her doing all the things her new baby sister was doing.

"Will you excuse me a minute?"
Sister said when the last video
had ended.
"I suppose so," said Mama as she watched
Sister scurry up the stairs and into her room.

"What do you think?" asked Mama.
"I think we'd better go see what
she's up to," said Papa.

Mama, Papa, and Brother sneaked up the stairs to see what Sister was up to. What she was up to was drawing another picture of the Bear family.

This is what it looked like:

My Family

Mama Papa Brother Sister Honey

Mama, Papa, and Brother breathed a sigh of relief. "It's just about bedtime, dear," said Mama. "We may as well start getting ready for bed."

"Mama," said Sister, "could we take a peek at the baby first?"

"I don't see why not," said Mama.

The Bear family tiptoed very quietly into the baby's room. Sister peeked through the bars of the crib at her sleeping baby sister.

"You know something?" she whispered.
"She *is* kind of cute."